# The Little Mermaid

Illustrated by Alan Marks

Retold by Katie Daynes
Based on a story by Hans Christian Andersen

Deep, deep down

below the ocean waves

lived the Sea King and his six mermaid daughters.

Each mermaid had her own sea garden.

The eldest made hers
in the shape of a whale.

The second mermaid made a pretty shell border.

And the third grew
bright, exotic sea flowers.

The fourth and fifth mermaids loved exploring.
So, they decided to fill their gardens
with treasure from shipwrecks.

The littlest mermaid found a statue of a prince.
"I'm going to put him in my garden,"
she said.

Each night, as the castle waters turned inky black,
the Sea King's mother called the mermaids inside.

"Tell us a story, Grandmama!" begged the mermaids.

"Tell us about the world above the waves."

"They have buildings as high as the ocean is deep," she said,

"and people with two legs and no tail..."

The little mermaid longed to see this world for herself,
but she had to wait for her sixteenth birthday.

Until then, she could only dream of sky
and air and people with two legs.

One by one, as the mermaids reached their
sixteenth birthdays, they were allowed to
glide to the ocean surface.

With the tips of their tails the mermaids touched the dry sand,
then they swam home, giggling with delight.

Eventually, only the little mermaid was left behind.

"What's your world like?" she asked her statue.

Finally, the year...

then the month...

then the day of the little mermaid's sixteenth birthday arrived...

...and she rose to the shimmering surface as quickly as she could.

As her head broke through the waves, she gasped.

The setting sun was spilling its light onto the water...
and there, ahead, floated a ship.

On deck, people with two legs danced and sang.

As she watched,
a young prince
appeared.

He's like my statue
...only alive.

Suddenly, a wild wind whipped up the waves.
Terrified passengers were tossed into the sea.

"I must help the prince!"
thought the little mermaid.

She dived through the waves until she found the prince

clinging to a broken mast.

Gently, the little mermaid towed him to a sheltered cove, where a wave washed him safely to shore.

Then she hid behind a rock and watched. A pretty girl came by.

She helped the prince to his feet and together they walked away.

"If only I had legs," sighed the little mermaid.

The little mermaid told her sisters about the prince.

"He lives in a grand marble palace by the cliffs," said one.

The eldest sister was worried.
"He's a man and you're a mermaid.
This will only make you unhappy."

The next evening the Sea King held a
magnificent summer ball.

The guests streamed in wearing
shimmery clothes.

Everyone swayed to the fish
band's songs... except for the
little mermaid. She couldn't stop
thinking about the prince.

"I must find him," she decided. "But first I need legs.

Maybe the sea witch can help me."

So she set out on a
dangerous journey to the
sea witch's cave.

The witch was waiting for her.
"So you want legs to impress
a prince," she cackled.

"Yes please," whispered
the little mermaid.

"Then I will need your voice for my potion," said the witch.
"If you win the prince's love, you will speak again."

"But if you fail,
        you must return to the sea and live in silence."

"I will not fail," said the little mermaid. Those were her last words.

By dawn, the little mermaid was sitting on a rock near the prince's palace.

She put the witch's potion to her lips and swallowed it in one gulp.

Her tail split in two

and she fell into the water.

The prince heard the
splash as she fell.
"Help that girl!" he ordered.

He asked her name, but the little mermaid could only smile.

The prince smiled back
and invited her to stay.

For the next few days, the little
mermaid lived in a dream.

"Once, I nearly drowned," said the prince.
"A beautiful princess rescued me. Tomorrow, I will set sail to marry her."

The prince's words were like a dagger in the mermaid's heart.

It was me.
I rescued you.

She could only watch as
the prince set sail for
his wedding.

"I have failed," thought the little mermaid,
tears streaming down her cheeks.

"Come to us,"
sang the ocean spray.

"Forever,"
whispered the foaming surf.

The sea rose up around the little mermaid

and she disappeared into the welcoming waves.

Edited by Jenny Tyler and Lesley Sims
Designed by Louise Flutter and Katarina Dragoslavic
Cover design by Russell Punter